"There's a very romantic side to me that you never saw, Emily," Shep said. *"You like candles and flowers, don't you, Em?"*

"Of course. What woman doesn't? I just never pictured you giving it a moment's thought."

"The matching half coins we exchanged on our wedding night were rather romantic," he said, giving her a quick glance.

"Yes, they were."

He moved close to her. "Where's your half of the coin, Em?" He reached inside his sweatshirt and pulled his chain out. "My father had mine, and I put it back on the minute he returned it to me. It's what they used as proof of my death, wasn't it?"

"Yes," she whispered, her gaze locked to his.

"Well, it's back around my neck, proof of my life with you. Where's yours, Em?" He slipped his fingers inside the top of her blouse. "Ah, Emily," he said as he felt the gold chain. He lifted it out and placed the coin in his hand, watching the sunlight dance across the shiny surface. "Did you ever take it off? When you filed for divorce, when you thought I was dead, did you take it off?"

Sudden tears misted her eyes. She shook her head, unable to speak.

"Oh, my Emily. My love. I love you so much, and seeing this chain around your neck means more to me than I can ever tell you." He lowered his lips toward hers. "Thank you. . . ."

WHAT ARE *LOVESWEPT* ROMANCES?

They are stories of true romance and touching emotion. We believe those two very important ingredients are constants in our highly sensual and very believable stories in the *LOVESWEPT* line. Our goal is to give you, the reader, stories of consistently high quality that may sometimes make you laugh, sometimes make you cry, but are always fresh and creative and contain many delightful surprises within their pages.

Most romance fans read an enormous number of books. Those they truly love, they keep. Others may be traded with friends and soon forgotten. We hope that each *LOVESWEPT* romance will be a treasure—a "keeper." We will always try to publish

LOVE STORIES YOU'LL NEVER FORGET
BY AUTHORS YOU'LL ALWAYS REMEMBER

The Editors

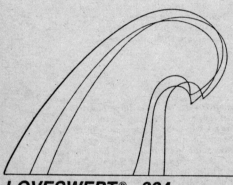

LOVESWEPT® • 324

Joan Elliott Pickart
To First Be Friends

B O O K S T O R E
952 West Prince Rd.
Tucson, Ariz. 85705
887-2112

BANTAM BOOKS
TORONTO • NEW YORK • LONDON • SYDNEY • AUCKLAND

TO FIRST BE FRIENDS

A Bantam Book / May 1989

*LOVESWEPT® and the wave device are registered
trademarks of Bantam Books, a division of
Bantam Doubleday Dell Publishing Group, Inc.
Registered in U.S. Patent
and Trademark Office and elsewhere.*

*If you would be interested in receiving protective vinyl
covers for your Loveswept books, please write to this address
for information:*

*Loveswept
Bantam Books
P.O. Box 985
Hicksville, NY 11802*

ISBN 0-553-21988-X

Published simultaneously in the United States and Canada

---

*Bantam Books are published by Bantam Books, a division
of Bantam Doubleday Dell Publishing Group, Inc. Its trademark, consisting of the words "Bantam Books" and the
portrayal of a rooster, is Registered in U.S. Patent and
Trademark Office and in other countries. Marca Registrada.
Bantam Books, 666 Fifth Avenue, New York, New York 10103.*

PRINTED IN THE UNITED STATES OF AMERICA

O   0 9 8 7 6 5 4 3 2 1

For Carolyn Nichols,
who made it all happen
way back when

Prologue

"Padre! Padre!"

The old priest stepped out of the crude hut to find a young wide-eyed boy racing toward him.

"Slow down, Pepee," the priest said, smiling, "or you'll knock me over like a bony cow on the road. What has you so excited?"

The boy stopped in front of him, gasping for breath. "There," he said, pointing to the thick jungle beyond the village. "*Vi un hombre grande que . . .*"

"English, Pepee, speak English," the priest instructed. "You saw a big man who—all right, who what?"

"Is on the ground, much hurt, much blood, Padre."

"Dear God," the priest said. "Pepee, go for your father and uncle and bring them to me. Then you can show us where the man is. Quickly. Run."

"*Sí, sí,*" Pepee said, dashing away.

A short time later the priest and the two other men were hurrying after Pepee, who ran ahead, urging them to go faster. They followed a trail into the jungle, but Pepee soon veered into the thick growth, forcing the others to brush aside the branches that swatted at their clothes. Then, in the grass beneath a tall tree, they saw him.

The man was lying on his back, his eyes shut, clothes dirty and torn. His right leg was covered in dried blood, his hair was matted, his face half-covered by a grimy beard.

"*Dios,*" Pepee's father said. "He is dead, yes?"

The priest dropped to his knees beside the injured man and placed his fingertips on the man's neck. "He's alive, but his pulse is very weak. Help me carry him to my hut."

Pepee's uncle hesitated. "Padre, we're isolated from everything because the monsoons have swollen the river, and more rain is coming. There's no way to get the man to a doctor. Never has the river been so high. We could be cut off here for weeks, months."

"Then we'll tend to him ourselves the best we can," the priest said. "Help me lift him."

"Who is he, do you think, Padre?" the other man asked.

"I don't know. There were rumors that the rebels had captured an American. I can only guess that he's the one, and he managed to escape. If that's true, he's come a long way through the jungle with that wound." The priest slid his arms beneath the man's shoulders to grip him around the chest. "Each of you lift one of his legs. Gently, now. We mustn't start the bleeding again. He's very weak."

"And very big," Pepee's father said with a grunt as the three hoisted their burden off the ground.

The unconscious man groaned once, then was silent as the men, breathing heavily from the effort, carried him slowly back to the village. In the priest's hut they laid him on a straw mat on the floor.

"He will not live," the uncle said, sweating profusely. "His breathing is not good, and I think he has a fever."

"I'll do all I can for him," the priest said, "and add prayers to my small supply of medicine. If it is meant to be, he will live." He began to remove the man's tattered clothes.

"Americans are very big," Pepee commented, peering at the man, awe evident in his voice.

The man groaned again, then mumbled something. The priest put his ear close to the man's mouth. He mumbled again, then was quiet.

"What did he say?" Pepee's father asked.

"He said 'Emily,' " the priest said softly. " 'Emily.' "

One

Emily hummed softly as she crossed the living room to the floor-to-ceiling windows that formed one entire wall. The view was breathtaking—a sunset etching vivid streaks across the sky, then seeming to merge with the ocean that stretched to the horizon. The beach was deserted, since people had gone for dinner in their homes dotting the shore.

Emily drank in the sight of nature's beauty for a long moment before switching her gaze to the drafting table that stood in front of the windows. She nodded in satisfaction, pleased with the drawings of elegant dresses she'd done that day. She was ahead of schedule on her assignment and Clare, her agent, would be delighted if the promised work arrived before expected.

Then, Emily thought, smiling, Clare would nag

until she agreed to take on the next project. "Emily Tyson," Clare would say, "your work is in demand, you're making a name for yourself at last. You can't pass up these prestigious jobs. Sit, draw, and hush." Clare was a dear, her friend as well as her agent, and Emily was grateful to have someone who sincerely cared about her, not just as an artist, a commodity, but as a person and a woman as well.

And there was Marilee, Emily mused, looking out the window again. Living alone next door, Marilee was in her mid-fifties, plump but didn't care, had been widowed for twenty-two years, and treated Emily like the daughter she had always yearned for. She fussed and clucked over Emily, continually told her she worked too hard, and showed up regularly with casseroles brimming with fresh vegetables and choice chunks of meat.

Emily sighed a contented, peaceful sigh, and a feeling of well-being swept over her. She'd fought hard and long for this sense of rightness in her life. It had been a difficult road, filled with many doubts and seemingly endless tears. Memories still haunted her at times, creeping into her mind with insistent fingers in the darkness of night. Tears would flow yet again, and she'd be overcome with loneliness as images of what once had been danced before her eyes.

But she'd gather her inner strength, dash the tears from her cheeks, and concentrate on the new day that would come with the dawn. Look forward, she would tell herself, not back. Think of the future, not the past. And then she would sleep, having conquered the ghosts and the memories once more.

Emily slipped the drawings into a folder and looked out the window again, watching the sunset melt into the ocean like softening butter. Darkness would soon fall. She moved around the drafting table to pull the burnt orange drapes over the windows, then turned and started across the room, turning on the television as she passed it. She was trying to decide what to make for her dinner when the brisk voice of the television announcer interrupted the regular program for a special news bulletin.

Emily gave full attention to the television screen.

"We switch you now to Bob Williams," the announcer continued, "at the State Department. Bob?"

"I've just come from a press conference," the newsman said, "that was called at the direction of the Secretary of State. Our government has received word that Shepherd 'Shep' Templeton, who was declared dead over six months ago, reportedly killed by rebels in Pataguam, is very much alive."

"What?" Emily whispered, her heart racing beneath her breast. She reached out blindly to grip the arm of a chair, then sank onto it heavily, her trembling legs refusing to hold her another moment.

"Shep Templeton," the newsman went on, "was, is a world-famous journalist who traveled to hotspots around the globe to gather information for his award-winning stories. Over six months ago Pataguam rebels boasted that they had killed him after capturing him in the jungles of Pataguam about two months after his arrival there. All efforts on the part of the State Department to secure the release of Templeton's body failed. The rebels sent, through underground channels, a gold chain from which hung half of a gold coin as proof of Templeton's death. Senator Shepherd Templeton, Senior, identified the chain and coin as belonging to his son, and Shepherd Templeton, Junior, was declared officially dead. A memorial service was held here in the nation's capital."

Without realizing she was doing it, Emily's fingers curled around the gold chain at her neck and pulled it free. Her other hand grasped the half of a gold coin that hung from it. Her eyes were riveted on the television, yet she felt totally disoriented, as though she were watching from afar, floating outside her own body.

"But Shep Templeton was *not* dead," Bob Williams continued. "He escaped from his captors shortly after he was seized. Badly wounded in the effort, he made his way through the jungles of Pataguam to the edge of a small village that was cut off for months by the monsoon flood waters. There he was nursed back to health by a priest and the villagers. Because of the floods, there was no way to communicate with the outside world during the months of Templeton's recovery."

"Shep?" Emily said, tears spilling down her cheeks. "Shep?"

"Templeton," Bob said, "was at last able to leave the village when the waters receded and he made his way across Pataguam until he arrived at a United

States Army post on the perimeter of the small, volatile country. A coded message was immediately sent to high-ranking officials at the Pentagon, who in turn notified the State Department. Senator and Mrs. Templeton were immediately informed that their son was alive. Shep Templeton is, at this moment, being flown home to Washington, D.C., where he will be given a complete physical at Walter Reed Army Medical Center, after which he will be debriefed by high-ranking officials. It is rumored that the President has expressed the wish to speak privately with Templeton."

A picture of Shep flashed on the screen, and Emily gasped. She started to rise, as though to go to him, but her attempt to leave the chair failed.

"Oh, Shep," she called, staring at the screen. There he was. Yes, it was Shep, smiling that boyish smile of his, his straight white teeth accentuating his deep tan. His features were rugged, creating an earthy handsomeness that made women's heads turn whenever he entered a room. Sensuous lips, square jaw, straight nose, deep brown eyes. And his hair—light brown, but streaked by the sun to near-blond, and needing a trim, as always. He was so tall, his shoulders so wide. "You're alive. You're alive," she said, nearly choking on a sob. She stumbled to her feet and moved to the set.

The picture of Shep disappeared, and Bob Williams was once more on the screen. "We'll have more details as they develop," he said "and the press corps—"

Emily turned off the set. Silence descended over the room, but a cacophony of voices screamed in

Emily's head. She wrapped her arms around herself, and swayed unsteadily on her feet.

Shep was alive, she thought over and over again. The only man she had ever loved wasn't dead, he was alive. The man she had been married to for three years was alive. The man she had told eight months before, when he refused to give up his plans to go to Pataguam, that she was divorcing him, was alive.

"Oh, dear heaven, that night," Emily said, pressing her hands to her pale cheeks. She edged to the sofa and sat down, reliving yet again that fateful night.

"You're going to do what?" Shep nearly yelled, narrowing his eyes.

"You heard me, Shep. I can't live like this anymore," Emily said, "not knowing how long you'll be home, where you'll go when, if you'll be alive one day to the next. If you go to Pataguam, I'm going to file for a divorce. I'm not living, I'm existing for the fleeting time we have together before you leave again. In the three years we've been married, we've spent together what amounts to a few weeks."

Shep flung a shirt into the duffel bag he was packing. "You knew what my work entailed when you married me."

"And I was foolish enough to believe that our love, what we have together, would be more important, would show you that you could have a prestigious career without putting yourself in continual danger. I was such a child, I was con-

vinced you'd change and want to be with me. But I've grown up in these three years, Shep. You are who you are. I love you, but I can't, I won't, live like this anymore. I'm going to get a divorce."

"No!" He crossed the room and pulled her into his arms. "Emily, don't do this. We'll talk when I get back, work something out. I love you, you know that."

Tears filled her eyes and she nodded as she wrapped her arms around his waist. "Yes, I know you do, but it's not enough. Our love for each other just isn't enough. We have different goals, needs, dreams." Sobs choked off her words, and her tears stained his shirt. "I can't live like this."

He wove his fingers through her short dark curls, and tilted her head back, seeing her shimmering blue eyes and the pain etched on her delicate features.

"We'll talk when I get back, Emily."

She shook her head. "You just got home from Israel. You promised we'd go away on the honeymoon we never had."

"We will, but things have exploded in Pataguam before anyone expected them to. I can't predict the timing of these things. You know that, you know I have to be in on the ground floor in order to write the stories I do. Our trip is just postponed, honey. When I come back—"

"I won't be here," she interrupted. She lifted her quivering chin. "I'm divorcing you, Shep. I have to, to save my sanity."

"Dammit, Emily, is a divorce decree, a piece of paper, going to turn off, like a faucet, what you feel for me? This is crazy. We love each other."

"You don't let that love stand in your way when you leave time and again."

"I have to go!"

"And I have to have a chance to build a life for myself that doesn't keep me in a state of fear for your life. Yes, I love you, and maybe I always will, but I don't like you. I don't like what you so uncaringly put me through when you pack that duffel bag and go out that door. When we wrote our wedding vows we said we'd always be each other's best friend as well as husband and wife. You're not my best friend anymore, you're my tormentor. My heart breaks a little more each time you go. It's over, Shep. It's over."

"No," he said with a strangled groan, then his mouth came down hard on hers.

Emily blinked as the living room of the beach house came back into focus. She drew a deep, shuddering breath, remembering that night with crystal clarity.

Shep's kiss had worked its magic as it always did, and she had succumbed to the want of him, tears still streaming down her face. There had been a frantic quality to his lovemaking that night, as though he wanted the power of his body to erase the horror of her words. She had received him eagerly, knowing it would be the last time, knowing she had to be free of this man she loved before he destroyed her.

And then he had gone.

She'd lain in bed, naked beneath the sheet, watching him dress, then quickly finish packing. He'd kissed her once more, his dark eyes blazing with intensity.

"Be here when I get back, Em. Please, be here. We'll talk, work this out, I swear it."

She'd said nothing. She'd simply looked at him with pain-filled eyes, and then he'd turned and strode from the room.

Her heart aching, she'd started divorce proceedings the day after. Official papers were channeled through the State Department, which was the normal procedure for Shep's mail whenever he went overseas since his work had proven to be valuable to the government as well as bringing Shep fame and wealth. But two months after he left, before the divorce was final, word came that he had been killed by the Pataguam rebels.

Never had Emily felt such devastating pain. As though moving in a trance, she instructed her attorney to finalize the divorce through whatever legal maneuvering it required. She would not be the recipient of Shep's property, his assets, his life insurance. It would be dishonest, wrong. Reporters hounded her, but she spoke to no one. Instead, she released a simple statement announcing that she and Shep were divorced, she was not legally his widow, and she had nothing further to say. Knowing that the senior Templetons had never approved of Shep's marriage to her, she'd left Washington, D.C., without contacting them.

Emily glanced around the room. She'd put the entire country between herself and her memories of her marriage to Shep. She'd bought the beach house on the California coast with the money she'd earned from her drawings. Shep had always insisted that she keep that money separate, that it was hers, and he would provide for her needs. She'd taken back her maiden name and begun to rebuild her shattered life and broken dreams. Not even dear Marilee knew who she really was. Only Clare, her agent, was aware that Emily Tyson was really Emily Tyson Templeton.

She buried her face in trembling hands, then dropped them to rest protectively on her protruding stomach, feeling the baby move beneath her palms.

Shep slammed the glass onto the bar and turned to face his parents, a deep frown on his face. The flames from the fire burning in the hearth cast a glow over his massive body, causing the half gold coin on the chain around his neck to shimmer. His father had returned the chain to him, and Shep had immediately slipped it over his head, welcoming its familiarity.

"What do you mean, you have no idea where Emily is?" he asked, nearly shouting.

"Shep, dear, please," Margaret Templeton said,

"you're exhausted. You just flew in late yesterday; you've had a grueling day with the doctor and the government officials. You need to rest. You weren't limping when you arrived yesterday, but now you are, which indicates that you've overdone. This is the first chance we've had to be alone with you. Can't we all just relax a bit before you go to bed?"

"No, Mother," he said tightly, "we cannot relax a bit. I want to know where Emily is."

"Darling, she divorced you," Margaret said.

"I'm aware of that. Preliminary papers reached me before I was captured. What you don't seem to understand is that I never agreed to that divorce. As far as I'm concerned, she's still my wife."

"Legally, she isn't," his mother pointed out. "Time passed. You couldn't contest, so the divorce became final."

"I don't give a hoot in hell about what's legal," Shep said even louder. "In my mind, in my heart, she's my wife, and I love her. I intend to find her and get this straightened out between us."

Margaret shook her head. "That's foolish. Emily obviously no longer loves you."

"Yes, she does," he said quietly. He sat in a leather chair by the fire, then absently rubbed his aching right thigh. "I know she does."

"I agree with you," Senator Templeton said. He sat in the matching leather chair opposite his son. "The fact that Emily proceeded with the divorce rather than reap the financial gains as your widow tells me a great deal."

"She divorced our son, Shepherd," Margaret insisted, leaning forward in her chair. "That's the point you should be focusing on. If you love a man, you certainly don't end your marriage to him."

"Yes, you do," Shep said, staring into the flames. "You do if the love wasn't enough because the marriage itself brought you nothing but heartache. Believe me, I've had many months to sort through this and I've been able to see it from Emily's viewpoint. I failed her as a husband. She had to divorce me because I left her no choice."

"That's absurd," Margaret said, smoothing the skirt of her raw silk dress.

Shep leaned his head back on the soft leather of the chair and sighed wearily. "No, it's not. There's nothing absurd about doing whatever you have to in order to survive. That's something else I've learned over the past months."

Margaret clicked her tongue. "Shep, really, there is no comparison between your marriage and what you endured in that jungle."

"Hell has many forms, Margaret," the senator said. "We're to blame for some of this. Emily was never comfortable around us. She wasn't made to feel welcome in this home. I, too, have had many months to think. We believed that our son was dead, but we also lost the daughter we could have had in Emily. We didn't even contact her when Shep's death was announced. We, my dear, are social snobs. Emily's parents were Iowa farmers. They were killed when she was fourteen and she lived in foster homes. Ah, yes, such a terrible background for the wife of Senator Templeton's son. How disgraceful that Emily's blood is red instead of society blue."

Surprise evident on his face, Shep lifted his head to look at his father. "I'm not sure I'm hearing this."

"It's long overdue," Senator Templeton said. "When I thought you were dead, son, I looked deep inside myself, taking stock of who I am. I can't say I was overly pleased with what I discovered."

"Shepherd," Margaret announced, "I am not a snob."

"Yes, Margaret," the senator replied calmly, "you are."

"Well!" she said indignantly. "I'm being insulted in my own home."

"That can't be helped." The senator shrugged his shoulders. "You listen to me, Margaret Templeton. If Shep wins back his Emily, that little girl is going to be the daughter we never had. She's going to feel welcomed and loved here, do you understand me?"

"Goodness—" Margaret nervously patted her perfectly coiffured gray hair "—you're certainly being . . . macho, Shepherd. I've never seen you like this. I—I give you my promise that I will welcome Emily into our home if, well, if she chooses to come."

"First," Senator Templeton said, "she has to be found. Shep, I know you have never used your last name, or my connections, to further your career. I've respected you greatly for that. However, I think this is one time you should put aside your pride and let me set the wheels in motion to find Emily. I give you my word that neither your mother nor I will interfere once Emily's whereabouts are discovered. At that point you'll be entirely on your own."

Shep leaned forward and rested his elbows on his knees, making a steeple of his fingers as he stared at his father. Several silent minutes passed before Shep spoke.

"I accept your offer of help," he said. "I'm afraid that Emily might move on from wherever she is now. She knows I'm alive. It's headline news across the country, which is ridiculous in itself. Eight months. I haven't seen her in eight months. Yes, Dad, pull out the stops, call in some favors, do whatever you have to, but find her."

"Oh, my darling boy," Margaret said, "you do love her so very much, don't you?"

"Yes, Mother, I do. I just hope I can convince her to give me another chance. I've changed. Those months in Pataguam made me realize I had my priorities all wrong. I abused the love Emily gave to me so openly, honestly, willingly. She trusted me, and I betrayed that trust. I was selfish, self-centered, and took her for granted. In short, if she shoots me on sight, I wouldn't blame her a bit."

Senator Templeton chuckled. "Yes, you *have* changed. And so have I."

"Well, I'm working on it," Margaret said. "But I'll need a little time to catch up with you two."

"Sad, isn't it?" Shep said. "I had to nearly die before I got a handle on what a total jerk I was."

"And I had to believe you were dead," the senator said, shaking his head. "Well, better late than never."

"It can't be too late for me and Emily," Shep said, his voice slightly husky. He looked into the flames again. "It just can't." He cleared his throat roughly, then got to his feet. "I think I'll turn in. It's been a long day. It's nice to know I have a comfortable bed waiting for me upstairs since Emily put all our furniture in storage and sent the key to the storage building to my attorney. He gave me a list of the inventory. Emily took nothing with her that had been ours. Nothing. Not even the rocking chair she'd always wanted that I gave to her on her twenty-sixth birthday last year. I can see her so clearly in my mind, sitting in that rocker. She is so incredibly beautiful."

"Go to bed, son," Senator Templeton said gently. "You're out on your feet."

"You're right. Listen, thank you, both of you. These months have been rough for you, too, and I'm sorry about that. But I'm grateful for the changes that have taken place within us."

"And we're grateful that you're alive and well, darling," Margaret said.

"He won't be if he doesn't get some rest," the senator said. "I'll start making those calls in the morning, son. We'll find your Emily. Go get some rest now."

Shep chuckled and started forward, cringing as a hot pain shot through his thigh and radiated up his back. "Hell of a day," he mumbled, limping out of the room.

In the room where he'd slept as a boy, Shep lay in bed, his hands laced under his head as he stared up into the darkness. The throbbing ache in his leg was forgotten as his thoughts centered on Emily. It had been the images of her in his mind that had kept him going through the steamy jungle after his escape. He'd pushed on despite the pain, the weakness, and the fever that clouded his brain, telling himself that each step he took would bring him closer to holding Emily in his arms.

Emily.

Where was she, he wondered frantically. He'd been filled with rage when he'd received the papers saying she'd filed for a divorce. Rage that had slowly changed over the months to hurt, emptiness, then finally understanding. At thirty-three he had grown up and realized that a man was accountable for his actions, that there was, indeed, a piper to pay.

He'd changed, but the tremendous task of convincing Emily stood before him like an enemy. No, he would win, he had to. But first he had to find her.

"Where are you, Em?" he asked the darkness. "What are you thinking now that you know I'm alive?"

His mind flitted back in time to that last night they'd had together. He saw Emily's tears, heard her sobs of despair. He'd made love to her roughly, urgently, desperately trying to replace her tears with the beautiful lovemaking they'd always shared. She'd welcomed him, clung to him, matched his pounding rhythm as she'd chanted his name like a litany. He'd been so sure they'd reaffirmed their commitment that night when, in actuality, Emily had been saying good-bye. She had called him her tormentor, and damn his soul, he'd listened but hadn't heard.

Shep pulled his hands from beneath his head and dragged them down his face. It wasn't over, he thought fiercely. It couldn't be. Dear God, he loved Emily with every breath in his body. He would be her best friend again, her husband, lover.

His hand closed over the half gold coin nestled on his chest. What had Emily done with hers, he wondered. They'd slipped the chains on each other's necks on their wedding night, and neither had removed them once during the three years they'd been together. Emily had understood that it was dangerous for a man as active as he to wear a ring that might get caught and tangled, causing serious injury. She'd worn a simple gold wedding band; his hand was bare. And so the matching halves of the coin. They were a visible, tangible sign of the commitment they'd made for a lifetime.

"Where's your half of the coin?" he whispered. "And your wedding band? And, Lord, Emily, where are *you*?"

With a sigh that was more of a moan, Shep closed his eyes and slowly gave way to the fatigue that was so great it caused his muscles to tremble. He slept, his dreams plagued by swirling images of Emily, who was running through a thick jungle, just beyond his reach. He saw the gold chain slip from her neck and catch on a sudden wind that swept it into oblivion. Emily ran on.

Shep woke with a start, drenched in sweat, his leg throbbing. The clock on the nightstand read four-twelve A.M. He had no desire to fall asleep again for fear that the dream would recur.

He lay perfectly still, focusing on one thought, one image, one vision.

Emily.

Two

During the following days Shep grew increasingly edgy and restless as he waited impatiently for some word about Emily from his father's sources. Offers flooded in from talk shows, local and national, and there was a constant string of telephone calls from reporters requesting interviews. Shep, much to his dismay, had become the nation's new media sensation, and mail poured in to him, sent in care of Senator Templeton's office.

"This country is hungry for a hero," the senator said. "It makes the people feel united, pulled together by a common bond. You, son, are the man of the hour."

Shep had snorted in disgust and strode from the room, resulting in his stumbling over two huge canvas mailbags his father had had delivered to the house from his office. The walls of the Templeton home rang with Shep's expletives.

The final straw was a registered letter from the head of a Hollywood film studio expressing a desire to discuss the possibility of making a movie of Shep's adventure in Pataguam, with Shep taking a screen test to play himself.

"Are these people nuts?" Shep roared.

"I'd need a new dress for the Academy Awards night," Margaret said. "Something stunning."

"Fruitcakes," Shep mumbled. "You're all fruitcakes."

Margaret laughed in delight.

Unable to leave the house without being besieged by reporters, Shep finally issued a statement saying that once he was fully rested and had tended to personal business neglected during his absence, he intended to write a book about his experience. While his announcement started a flurry of telephone calls from publishers, it did cause the dejected reporters to move on, seeking other news.

Little was said about Emily in the stories being printed, other than to mention that Shep had been married for three years to the former Emily Tyson, but they were now divorced.

When Shep had been home for one week, which to him had seemed an eternity, Senator Templeton entered the house at the surprising hour of two in the afternoon. Margaret was out at a committee meeting, and the senator found his son staring moodily into a fire in the hearth in the living room. The late

October day was chilly, accompanied by a biting wind.

"Shep?" the senator called, walking slowly toward him.

Shep's head snapped around. "Hello, Dad. I didn't even hear you come in. Rather early for you, isn't it?"

"My people have found Emily," he said softly.

Shep stiffened and watched intently as the older man settled in the chair across from him. "You look upset. Why? Is something wrong with Emily?"

"No, no, she's fine."

"Where is she?"

"She purchased a beach house in California."

"California," Shep repeated slowly. "Well, she certainly put as many miles as she could between herself and the life we shared here. What else?"

"She's living in a nice area below Malibu, without Malibu prices. She's making quite a name for herself doing illustrations for fashion brochures and newspaper ads, designing several dresses for the female lead of a nighttime soap opera, and so on. She's using her maiden name, Emily Tyson."

"I see," Shep said. "She's totally disassociated herself from me, hasn't she? She's put an entire country between us and no longer uses my name."

"Shep, she thought you were dead."

"The world now knows that I'm alive," he said, his jaw tightening. "She's made absolutely no attempt to contact me or—but that's my problem. I assume you have her address?"

"Yes, but . . ." The senator's voice trailed off, and he sighed.

Shep leaned forward. "But? There's something else, isn't there? What aren't you telling me? Is it a man? Is Emily involved with someone?"

"No man has ever been seen going into her house. She has a neighbor lady she's friendly with, and her agent, Clare Fairchild, apparently drives up from Los Angeles to visit frequently."

"Clare? Yes, I met her once. She's been Emily's agent and close friend since before Em and I were married. My meeting with Clare was brief, but Emily spoke of her often. I should have remembered that and contacted Clare myself. Well, no matter. Emily has been found. Dad, why do I get the feeling you're holding something back?"

"Because I am," he said, throwing up his hands. "Shep, there's no easy way to say this, except to just say it. Emily is . . . is expecting a baby. She's pregnant."

Shep sank back in the chair as he stared at his father, a sudden pain at his temples. That last night, he concluded. He'd made love to Emily with no thought of taking precautions. She'd had adverse physical reactions to the Pill, so they'd agreed to share the responsibility of birth control, alternating between them. But not that last night. Neither one of them had considered it in the emotionally charged atmosphere. That was over eight months ago now.

Shep looked up at the ceiling for a long moment, hating himself for the question he was about to ask, but knowing he had to have the answer. He redirected his tormented gaze to his father. "How . . . far along is she in her pregnancy?" His voice was gritty. "When is the baby due?"

"I don't know."

"Dammit, Dad," he said, smacking the arm of the chair with his hand, "I *have* to know. If she's over eight months pregnant, then that baby is mine. But if she's not that far along then . . . Dear God"—he ran a trembling hand down his face—"then she's been with another man. Why in the hell didn't your super-sleuths find out when that baby is due?"

"It's not that easy. A stranger can't waltz into a doctor's office and casually ask when Mrs. Tyson's baby is expected to arrive."

"*Mrs.* Tyson?"

"She's established herself in the area as a widow. I imagine she added the 'Mrs.' for the child's sake. Now, listen to me. My men have seen Emily. They report that she appears to be in the advanced stage of pregnancy. Advanced stage, Shep."

"Advanced stage? What in the hell does that mean?"

"It means," Margaret said, walking into the room, "that she feels like a whale, her feet are a forgotten entity that she hasn't seen in a while, she's uncomfortable, can't sleep well, and has to go to the bathroom every two minutes. It also means she is often very frightened."

"Frightened?" Shep echoed, stiffening in the chair again.

Margaret rolled her eyes heavenward. "Of course

she's frightened, young man. You just participated in the pleasurable part, then you zipped your pants and walked away."

"Mother, for heaven's sake," Shep said, feeling heat rise along his neck.

Senator Templeton chuckled. "Do continue, Margaret, you're on a roll."

"Damn right I am. I'll tell you this, Shepherd Templeton, Junior, carrying you for nine months was no picnic, and your father was with me every step of the way. When it came close to my due date, I wanted to cancel the whole thing. The thought of going through the pain of labor and birth made me shudder. But the pain was forgotten the moment I saw you, all eight pounds six ounces of you, screaming your lungs out. Up until then I was so terribly, terribly frightened. And I wasn't even alone. Emily has been alone through her entire pregnancy. God love her, I certainly wouldn't wish that on anyone."

"Shep doesn't know for a fact that this is his child," the senator pointed out.

Margaret sighed. "I'd like to rant and rave and say it doesn't matter, that if Shep loves her, he should go to her anyway. But . . . well, do you have the name of Emily's doctor, Shepherd?"

"Yes, it's in my briefcase on the entryway table."

Margaret spun around and marched from the room.

"She's something when she gets a bee in her bonnet," Senator Templeton said, laughing softly.

"Dad," Shep said, "I *am* going to Emily, no matter when that baby is due. You said there's no evidence of another man in her life now, so she's alone. If the baby isn't mine, we'll deal with that later, but I can't stand the thought of her having no one and being frightened."

The senator looked at his son for a long moment. "You're a hell of a man, Shep. You're doing the right thing, and I respect you very much for this decision. You realize, of course, that Emily might not be overjoyed to see you."

Shep nodded, but before he could reply, Margaret came back into the room.

"I should have been a detective," she said, sitting down in a chair upholstered in gray velvet. "I called Emily's doctor's office and spoke with the receptionist. I told her that I represented one of the firms that Emily does fashion drawings for, and we wanted to give her a gift of the services of a housekeeper for her first month home from the hospital. So I asked if she would be kind enough to give me Emily's approximate due date. And, of course, I told her not to breathe a word of it to Emily because it was a surprise. The girl thought that was the sweetest thing, and nearly fell over herself pulling Emily's file."

Shep got to his feet. "Mother, wait, don't say any more. I'm going out there to be with Emily no matter when that baby is due."

"My goodness," Margaret said, "I certainly did a superb job of raising you." Senator Templeton hooted with laughter. "By the way, I heard the entire conversation between you two because I was listening outside the door."

"Who raised *you*?" the senator asked.

"Mickey Spillane," she said. "Anyway, Shep, since it doesn't matter to you, I won't tell you when she's due." Then, beaming, she turned to her husband. "Shepherd, we are going to become grandparents in two weeks, give or take a few days. First babies are a tad unpredictable."

"Splendid," Senator Templeton said, matching her expression.

"What?"

Margaret rose and went to Shep, reaching up to place her hands on his cheeks. "That baby is yours. You're going to be a father, and I highly admire your gallant intentions. I realize I'm interfering, but you and Emily have so many obstacles in your path to overcome without your doubt about that baby's father. Emily was free to do with her life as she chose. To have had a relationship with another man would have been her business, but it would have hurt you deeply had it been true. This way, your determination will be twofold. You're fighting for your wife and for your child, with the hope that the three of you will share a future together."

"You're very wise, Mother," Shep said.

She dropped her hands from his face and smiled up at him. "Winning Emily back is going to call for patience on your part. That has never been one of your virtues, you know."

"I realize that. I'd like nothing better than to pound

on Emily's door, carry her off, and marry her again before our baby is born."

"Uh-oh," Senator Templeton said.

"Don't worry, Dad, I'm not that naive. I was foolish enough to think I could conduct my life as I always had when I married Emily. I made no concessions, no compromises, simply expected her to do all the adjusting, accept my life-style exactly as it was. Well, I lost my wife because of my actions. I have no intention of making the same mistakes again."

"I'm guilty of those attitudes too," Margaret said. "I just assumed that Emily would be eager to join my volunteer committees, help plan the socials and balls. When she chose to use her time to further her career, I stood in judgment of her, decided she wasn't performing as a Templeton should. Dear heaven, I hope she'll forgive me."

"We're in the background, Margaret," the senator pointed out. "Shep is up at bat first. He has a very difficult task ahead of him."

Shep ran his hand over the back of his neck. "That's no joke. I'm going to have to take this slow and easy. To first be friends, that's where I'll have to begin." He walked across the room. "I'm going to call the airlines and see how soon I can get a flight to California." He stopped and turned to look at his father. "Thanks for all you did to find Emily."

Senator Templeton nodded, then watched Shep leave the room. "Godspeed, son," he said quietly.

Margaret grasped her husband's hand. "Amen to that."

Emily sat on the end of the sofa, watching the dancing flames in the fireplace as she spoke into the telephone. "All is well, Clare. The doctor said the baby is starting to turn and drop a bit. He said it would be another two weeks. Of course, it could be a little sooner, or a little later."

"Oh, thanks," Clare said. "I want this pinpointed to the exact day and time so I can be there. I'm forty-two years old; I can't deal with this kind of stress."

"You're going to be a wonderful godmother, if you survive the birth of this baby," Emily assured her, smiling.

"You bet I will. The best godmother ever produced." She paused. "Emily, are you doing all right? Physically, yes, I know you're fat and fine, but what about mentally? It was a tremendous shock to you to learn that Shep is alive."

"Yes, it was," Emily said quietly, "but I've settled down now. I'm very grateful he wasn't killed, but he and I are divorced. We simply don't want the same things. Believe me, I'm not entertaining any fantasies about us getting back together."

"What about the baby? It *is* his child."

Emily sighed. "I know. After the baby is born and I'm back on my feet, I'll contact Shep, or maybe just his attorney, to see if Shep wants visitation rights. I couldn't begin to guess what Shep might say. During the years we were married, I brought up the subject of children countless times, but he always said he wasn't ready for that kind of responsibility. Between his constant travel and the fact that we now live on opposite coasts, I don't picture his having much time to visit his child. Clare, this baby is mine, and I intend to raise her alone."

Clare laughed. "There you go with the 'her' again. Brother, are you going to be in for a shock when you have a boy."

"Nope, it's a girl, I'm sure of it."

"Yes, Mother. I hear you, Mother. I've got to dash. I'll call you in a couple of days. Marilee is checking on you regularly, isn't she?"

"Goodness, yes. She's wonderful. I've decided to tell her the truth about who I am. She's been a dear friend, and I hate this subterfuge."

"Good. Now I won't have to worry about letting something slip when I'm there. Must go. Talk to you soon, sweets. 'Bye."

"Good-bye, Clare," Emily said, then replaced the receiver.

She glanced at her watch and saw that it was just after two o'clock. She had several hours before dinner, and could get some work done. But, oh, mercy, she was sleepy. The baby had been so active during the night, waking her often, and a short nap sounded absolutely delicious. Just a short one, there in front of that lovely fire.

She propped her feet on a footstool, shoved a throw

pillow behind her back, another under her head, and closed her eyes, her hands resting on her large stomach. Within moments she was asleep.

Shep turned into the driveway, shut off the ignition of the car he'd rented at the airport, then folded his arms on the top of the steering wheel as he scrutinized Emily's house.

Nice, he thought. Very nice. It was bigger than a cottage, but not enormous, probably had three bedrooms. It was painted white with dark blue shutters and trim, and a blue front door. Smoke was curling from the chimney, and Emily's red compact car was parked ahead of him in the driveway. All he had to do was get out of the car, cross the yard, and knock on the door. That's all he had to do to see the woman he loved, the woman who had filled his mind and heart for the past long, lonely eight months.

Except he was scared to death.

He'd known fear over the years from facing danger and death in remote places of the world. He knew how it tasted and felt, how it gripped a man's soul with an icy hand.

But this fear, he realized, was different. It was coming from another place within him—his heart. His strength, size, and cunning meant nothing. He felt stripped bare and vulnerable, totally defenseless against a delicate woman who held his future happiness in her hands. He'd never been in a position like this before, and he didn't like it, not one damn bit.

Easy does it, Templeton, he told himself. If he didn't get his act together, he'd blow this in the first five minutes.

He took a deep breath and let it out slowly, switching his gaze to the beach below the sloping incline beyond the house and to the endless stretch of water. A chill wind was blowing, and the ocean was a murky green with swirling whitecaps. The sky was gray, hinting at rain. It was a formidable scene but, yet, he could picture it bathed in sunlight, the water and sky calm and clear blue. Emily would like walking on that beach, her toes curling into the warm sand.

He could see her, too, he continued to muse, sitting on a blanket, smiling in delight as their child played with a pail and shovel. And where would *he* be, he wondered. Would he be welcomed on that blanket next to Emily, his love, his wife? Would they be watching their baby together, or would he be alone in Washington, having been sent away, relegated to the role of a visiting father like so many men he knew?

"No!" he said as he quickly got out of the car, and closed the door with more force than necessary.

Dammit, Templeton, he raged, calm down! He'd rehearsed his greeting over and over during the seemingly endless flight across the country. "Hello, Emily, fancy meeting you here." "Well, Em, I turned up, just like a bad penny." "Emily, I love you, you love me, so quit horsing around and marry me . . . again!" "So, Em, what's new? Besides the baby you're carrying that was fathered by me on the last night we were together."

Shep groaned and shook his head. He'd rehearsed all right, and rejected every phrase as asinine. Smooth-talking son of a gun that he supposedly was, he didn't know what to say to his own wife when she opened that door!

Ex-wife, a small inner voice taunted.

"Enough of this garbage," he said, squaring his shoulders. "Okay, Templeton, this is it."

He strode around the car, across the yard, up the two steps of the small porch, then made a fist and lifted it, ready to knock on the dark blue door. He looked at his fist, the door, then his fist again, which seemed frozen in place only inches from the wood panel.

"Do it," he ordered himself.

Emily awoke with a start, momentarily disoriented. She blinked, saw by her watch that it was nearly three, then wondered what had awakened her with such a jolt. There was a sharp knock at the door.

So that was it, she thought, lowering her feet to the floor and attempting to rise. She shifted her cumbersome body and tried again, managing to get off the sofa. "Such gracefulness," she scoffed.

She moved slowly across the room, feeling stiff and awkward, and yawned as she opened the door.

Everything seemed to stop.

Emily felt as though she were teetering on the

edge of time, suspended there, not breathing. Then the edge tilted, sliding her into the past she'd shared with the man standing before her. The rushing noise in her ears echoed his name over and over, louder than the biggest waves crashing onto the shore.

"Emily?"

The deep, rich timbre of the familiar voice reached out and touched her with a gentle hand, pulling her back to the present. The edge straightened, steadied, the rushing noise stilled, and she drew a deep breath of air into her lungs.

"Shep?" she asked, hardly above a whisper.

Shep didn't know what to do or say; he could only stand there drinking in the glorious sight of his beautiful Emily. There she was—with her short, silky dark curls that he used to tangle his fingers in . . . with her delicate features, her kissable lips, her big blue eyes that changed to nearly smoky gray when she was filled with desire. . . . Emily. His love, his life, his wife. Gazing at her small hands resting on the extended slope of her body that held their baby brought tears to his eyes. Dear heaven, he was home.

Shep? Emily's mind repeated. Yes, he was really there, so tall, massive, wearing jeans and a sheep-skin jacket. His hair was being tousled by the wind, the sun-streaked strands tumbling onto his tanned forehead. Still it needed a trim. There were tiny lines around his eyes that hadn't been there before, making him appear slightly older. What caused those lines? Fatigue? The pain he'd endured in the jungles of Pataguam?

No, no, she thought frantically, she didn't want him with her, not now. All her energies, her emotions, and strength had to be centered on her baby. Later she had intended to tell him of the child. But for now he had to go away, leave her alone, allow her the peace she needed to bring her baby safely into the world.

"Emily," Shep said, his voice husky with emotion, "may I . . . may I come in?"

Come in, she wondered hysterically. Into what? Her home? Her world? And, God help her, her heart? No! "No," she said, her voice sounding strange to her own ears. She pressed her hands more firmly onto her stomach as the baby shifted within her, kicking her with solid thumps. She drew in a sharp breath, glanced down at her swollen belly, then looked at Shep again. "No."

Shep's eyes followed the path of hers, lingering longer on the bulge beneath her hands before meeting her gaze again. "What's wrong?" he asked, frowning. "What happened? I heard you gasp. Are you in pain? Why did you take that quick breath as though you were hurt?"

"Nothing is wrong," she said crossly. "You'd gasp, too, if someone kicked you in the stomach. Shep, go away. I don't know how you found me, but I don't want to see you, or talk to you, not now."

"Dammit, that's my baby who just kicked you," he shouted. "I have every right to be here. Or weren't you intending to tell me about my own child?"

"Of course I was," she said, her voice rising. "I

was going to inform you after she was born. I don't have the energy for this now. Just leave me alone!"

"No! You're my wife and—"

"I'm not your wife!" she said fiercely. A chill wind whipped across the porch and she wrapped her arms around herself.

"You're freezing." Shep pushed the door open and moved into the room.

Emily turned to face him, her eyes flashing with anger. "You can't barge in here like you own the place."

"Move," he ordered, starting to close the door.

"No."

"Do you want to be carried inside?" he asked, narrowing his eyes.

"Oh, big macho deal. I weigh a lot more than I did the last time you picked me up and—" And carried her into their bedroom, where they'd made wondrous love. "I'm fat and heavy."

"I'll risk it," he said, starting to reach for her.

"No, don't touch me." She backed away several steps, then turned and stared at the flames in the fireplace across the room.

Don't touch me. The words reverberated in Shep's mind, causing a great pain, as if a sharp knife had twisted in his gut. He closed the door, seeing the trembling of his hand as he released the doorknob.

Seconds of oppressive silence passed, broken only by the faint crackle of the burning wood in the hearth.

"Emily, I . . ." Shep cleared his throat. "I'm sorry I

upset you," he said quietly. "I realize now that I should have called first and warned you I was coming." He paused. "No, maybe not. You might have disappeared before I could see you, talk to you."

She slowly turned her head to look at him. "This is my home. It's supposedly my safe haven. No one is capable of driving me away from here." She tore her gaze from his and went to the sofa, easing herself down.

Shep unbuttoned his jacket but didn't remove it as he looked around. Emily's safe haven, he thought. It was a lovely room. She'd decorated it in rich earth tones that created a warm, welcoming effect. The carpeting was thick, chocolate-brown, and he could picture it strewn with the toys of a happy, busy baby. The walls of this home would ring with a child's laughter, mingled with Emily's. And his?

Shep shook his head and dragged a restless hand through his windblown hair. This was going all wrong, he knew. It was as though he and Emily were meeting for the first time. They were wary, unsure of each other. And in a sad way, that was true. He loved Emily, but did he really know her? What were her hopes, dreams, whimsies, fantasies, her deepest, most secret wishes? He had to stay in her life so she could learn who he'd become, but more important so that he could discover Emily. Just loving her wasn't enough—she'd said that to him the night he'd left for Pataguam, and he'd finally come to understand during those months in the jungle. It just couldn't be too late for them to start over.

"Shep," Emily said, bringing him back from his tangled thoughts. She continued to stare into the fire, not turning her head to look at him. "Would you please leave?"

He sighed. "No, Em, I can't. I just can't."

"We have nothing more to say to each other," she said wearily. "It's all been said—countless times. Nothing has changed."

I've changed! he wanted to scream. But he couldn't say it yet, because she'd never believe him. She'd think it was just another implied promise he would break.

"May I take off my coat and sit down?" he asked.

"I'd prefer you to go."

Shep frowned at the back of her head, shrugged out of his jacket, and hung it on a peg by the door. He sat on the sofa, settling on the opposite end from Emily.

She glared at him. "Like I said, nothing has changed. You still do exactly as you please with no consideration for anyone else's wishes. This, Mr. Templeton, is *my* home. Not ours, mine."

"And that," he said, pointing at her stomach, "is *our* baby. Not yours, ours."

She lifted her chin. "Are you so certain of that? I thought you were dead, remember? Who's to say I didn't take a lover?"

Shep looked at her for a long moment before he spoke in a soft voice. "When I first learned that you were pregnant, all I could think about was when the baby was due, whether or not it was mine. You had to be eight months pregnant if I was the father."

"And if I was, say, six months along? What then?" she challenged him, looking directly into his eyes.

"My mother gave me a stiff lecture on what it would be like to go through pregnancy alone as you have."

"Your mother?" Emily said, surprise evident on her face. "Your parents don't even like me. Why would she be concerned? Never mind. That's not the issue at the moment."

"No, it's not. Em, I suddenly knew that I was coming here no matter when the baby was due. I couldn't stand the thought of you being alone, possibly frightened. If the baby wasn't mine, I'd deal with that later, but I was coming, and I wasn't leaving you to face another day of this by yourself. My decision on that was firmly made, *then* when she was sure I'd hear, my mother told my father the baby was due in two weeks. I know that baby is mine, ours. The point is, Emily, I'd be here whether that was the case or not."

Emily felt the sudden achy sensation of threatening tears in her throat. She believed every word that Shep had just said. How dare he do something so wonderful! It wasn't fair, not when her emotions had been on an unpredictable roller coaster for months now, and she never knew what would trigger a crying jag, or a dose of the blues, or a wave of fright.

"Well, that's very . . . nice, Shep, but I'm fine, as

you can see. Fat, but fine. I have friends looking after me, and a doctor whom I trust completely. You can fly out from D.C. once the baby is born and see her."

"I'm staying, Em."

She threw up her hands. "Well, I can't force you to go home, can't carry you bodily to the airport. There are some nice hotels and motels in the area where you can—"

"Whoa," he said, silencing her with a gesture. "You're not getting the drift of what I'm saying. I'm staying *here*, in this house, with you."

Emily's eyes widened. "You certainly are not. You seem to have forgotten that we're no longer married."

"Priority number one is our baby, Emily. We created it together, we'll be together when it's born. We'll get into all the other complexities of our lives later. Forget everything else for now, and concentrate on the fact that as the baby's father, I have the right to be here. You have a guest room, don't you?"

"Yes, but—"

"I'll get my luggage in before it gets any colder out there." He got to his feet.

"No, now, wait a minute. You can't—"

"Em, I want to be able to tell my son I was there when he was born. You wouldn't deny me that, would you?"

"It's a girl."

"Did you have that special test?"

"No, I just know it's a girl."

He started toward the door. "Bet you a buck it's a boy."

"Hold it, Shep. You're not staying in this house."

He stopped with his hand on the doorknob. "Yes, I am. Think about it, Em. Through the remainder of your pregnancy you're going to be pampered and looked after, and you're not going to be alone. Not anymore." He left the house.

"Not alone," Emily whispered. How heavenly that sounded. Even with Marilee nearby there had been times when Emily had felt so isolated, lonely, frightened. But now Shep was—

"No! Darn him, how did he do that? I didn't agree to this," she fumed. Nothing had changed where Shep Templeton was concerned. He most definitely still did exactly as he pleased. Well, she had a little surprise in store for him. She was going to pretend that he was invisible, totally ignore him, go about her business as though he weren't even there.

And he absolutely, positively, would never discover that she still loved him every bit as much as she always had.

Three

Thunder was rumbling across the sky as Shep got his luggage out of the trunk of the car. He realized with a chuckle that he felt as he had when he'd talked his way out of a narrow alley where three hoods had been ready to take him apart. Emily was a tough opponent, but he'd done it somehow—he was staying in the house with her. Despite the wall she had erected between them that was so real it was a wonder he couldn't feel it when he tried to approach her.

Shep started slowly toward the house, a frown now on his face. Emily really didn't want him there, he thought. Lord, that hurt. During the months they'd spent getting to know each other after meeting at a party in D.C., then through the years of their marriage, Emily had been his lifeline as he'd traveled far and wide to investigate for his stories. The knowledge that she was waiting for him to return had kept him going through more than one steamy jungle and frozen wasteland.

At least he was with her now. He'd noticed there was a glow about her, an indefinable something that, he supposed, came from her pregnancy. He'd heard that cornball stuff before, but now believed it might be true. God, there was a miracle nestled within her, a tiny baby created by the two of them; half her, half him. Incredible.

He was determined to be with her when their child was born. And then what? No, one step at a time here, slow and easy.

Shep reentered the house with his suitcases and pushed the door closed with his foot.

"The guest room is down the hall, first door on your right."

His head snapped around, and he saw Emily sitting on a stool in front of a drafting table. The chair had a high back, and she'd tucked a throw pillow behind her. She didn't look at him as she moved a pencil quickly across the paper in front of her. The light she'd turned on due to the lack of sunshine cast a circle of brightness around her, making her dark curls appear like shimmering silk.

Beautiful, Shep thought, then pulled his gaze from her and went in search of the guest room.

What he found was a good-size, pleasant room decorated in the same earth tones as what he'd seen of the rest of the house. There was a double bed, nightstand, dresser, a small desk, and a bathroom. Neither too feminine nor too masculine, it would welcome any guest.

Shep flung his luggage onto the bed and began to unpack. Guest, he thought in disgust. He was a guest in his wife's home. A guest was someone who was there temporarily, someone who came, then went.

He had to admit that he'd been a guest in the three years of his marriage to Emily. He came, then went, giving little notice of his arrivals and departures. And Emily had always been there to welcome him home and see him off. He'd taken it all for granted, including her love, used and abused the goodness of her without stopping long enough to realize what he was doing.

He opened the closet and hung up his shirts, pants, and jackets. Emily had sat him down on more than one occasion, he recalled, and asked him to please weigh and measure the trips he took, choose only the most important ones, compromise, bend a little.

He'd listened to her, but it wasn't until those months in Pataguam, when he'd replayed those conversations over and over in his mind, that at last he had gotten her message. Only then did he hear the tears in Emily's voice as she'd begged him to bring a reasonable balance to their lives. With shame he'd remembered the number of times they'd made plans for a honeymoon trip, then he'd canceled at the last minute to rush away to a foreign country to pursue a story. The honeymoon was simply postponed; that's what he'd always told her. Then Emily canceled the marriage itself when she had reached the end of her endurance.

Shep shook his head, then finished unpacking, placing the empty suitcases in the closet. It was all so clear to him now; his mistakes were flashing like neon signs. But how, he wondered, was he ever going to convince Emily he'd really changed?

He wandered back into the living room, accepted that Emily wasn't going to acknowledge his presence at the moment, then took another log from the wicker basket next to the fireplace and placed it on the fire. He settled onto the sofa and stretched his legs out in front of him, crossing them at the ankles. His thigh was aching from the long hours spent cramped in one position on the plane, and he rubbed his hand over the tight muscles as he stared into the dancing flames.

Emily watched Shep from beneath her lashes. He looked good in this room, she decided, in this house which suited her and, yet, also suited Shep, a big man, a powerfully sensual man.

There was such strength in that massive body, she mused, yet he was capable of such gentleness when he took her into his arms. Their lovemaking had always been exquisite, in tune. It seemed they'd known intuitively when the urgency of their passion would bring them together quickly, roughly, in frenzied need or when their bodies sought the slow, sensuous delights.

When he came to her, filled her, meshed their